First published 2007
Evans Brothers Limited
2A Portman Mansions
Chiltern Street
London W1U 6NR

Text copyright © Vivian French 2007
© in the illustrations Tim Archbold 2007

British Library Cataloguing in Publication Data

French, Vivian
    Growl! - (Spirals)
    1. Children's stories
    I. Title
    823.9'14[J]

ISBN-10: 0 237 53351 0 (hb)
ISBN-13: 978 0 237 53351 9   (hb)

ISBN-10: 0 237 53345 6   (pb)
ISBN-13: 978 0 237 53345 8 (pb)

Printed in China

Series Editor: Nick Turpin
Design: Robert Walster
Production: Jenny Mulvanny

GROWL!

Vivian French
and Tim Archbold

Evans

On the edge of the woods was a little blue house. Inside the house lived Mr and Mrs Wolf, Baby Wolf, and a GREAT BIG MONSTER who was very VERY fierce. Even at breakfast.

"Grrrr!" growled Wally the great big monster. "Grrr! Grrr! Grrr!"

"Wally," said his mother, "PLEASE stop growling. You're scaring your little sister."

Grrr!

Grrr!

"GRRR!" said Wally, even louder.

Wally's mother frowned. "Wally," she said, "if you don't stop growling THIS MINUTE you will NOT be allowed to go fishing."

Grrr!

Wally stopped growling and ate his breakfast. After he'd finished he went to find his fishing rod.

"Grrr!" he growled as he came to say goodbye.

Mrs Wolf sighed. "Have a lovely time, Wally dear," she said. "And be very careful."

"GRRRRRRR!" growled Wally, and he stamped off and away along the path.

On the other side of the woods
was a little red house.

Inside the house lived Mr and Mrs Bear, Baby Bear and a TERRIBLE SCARY CREATURE who was very VERY frightening. Even at breakfast.

"Grrr!" growled Bobbie. "Grrr! Grrr! Grrr!"

"Bobbie," said her dad, "You've been growling for days and DAYS and I'm tired of it.

Please stop RIGHT NOW, or you
can't go fishing."

Grrr!

Bobbie stopped growling and gobbled her breakfast. Then she jumped down from the table and went to find her fishing rod.

"Bobbie!" her dad called after
her. "Be careful! The pond is
very deep!"

"GRRRRRRR!" growled Bobbie
as she skipped down the path.

Wally stamped towards the pond.

"I'm the biggest monster in the whole wide world," he said to himself. "And I can scare ANYTHING!'

On the other side of the woods Bobbie was skipping towards the pond.

"I'm the scariest creature in the whole wide world," she said to herself. "And I can scare ANYTHING!"

Wally and Bobbie arrived at the pond together.
Wally looked at Bobbie.

Bobbie looked at Wally.

"Grrr!" said Wally.
Bobbie didn't move.

Grrr!

"Grrr!" said Bobbie.
Wally didn't run away.

Grrr!

Grrr!

"GRRR!" growled Wally.
"GRRR!" growled Bobbie.

Grrr!

"GRRR!" growled Wally.
"GRRR!" growled Bobbie.

They growled and they growled
and they GROWLED until they
were both out of breath...

...and then they looked at each
other ... and neither of them
moved and the wood
was VERY quiet until –

RIBBIT!

A frog jumped out of the pond.
"AAAAAAGH!" yelled Wally.
"OOOOOOH!" shrieked Bobbie.

And they both ran
home just as fast as they
could go.

"Are you still a big fierce monster?"
Wally's Mum asked.

"No," said Wally. "I'm a little wolf
and I want a hug."

"Are you still a terrible scary creature?" Asked Bobbie's Dad.

"No," said Bobbie. "I'm a little bear and I want a cuddle."

"Grrr," said Wally's little brother.
"Grrr. Grrr. GRR!"

Grrr!

"Grrr," said Bobbie's little sister.
"Grrr! Grr! GRR!'

Grrr!

Why not try reading a Spirals book?

Megan's Tick Tock Rocket by Andrew Fusek Peters,
Polly Peters, and Simona Dimitri
ISBN 978 0237 53342 7

Growl! by Vivian French and Tim Archbold
ISBN 978 0237 53345 8

John and the River Monster by Paul Harrison and Ian
Benfold Haywood
ISBN 978 0237 53344 1

Froggy Went a Hopping by Alan Durant and Sue Mason
ISBN 978 0237 53346 5